Sandy the Sloth
and the
Danger of Diablo

To Iris

"Hang in there"

David Otis

Sandy the Sloth
and the
Danger of Diablo

David Otis

BROWN BOOKS KIDS

Sandy the Sloth and the Danger of Diablo

Brown Books Kids
16250 Knoll Trail Drive, Suite 205
Dallas, Texas 75248
www.BrownBooksKids.com
(972) 381-0009

A New Era in Publishing®

Publisher's Cataloging-In-Publication Data

Names: Otis, David, 1956- author.
Title: Sandy the sloth and the danger of Diablo / David Otis.
Description: Dallas, Texas : Brown Books Kids, [2020] | Summary: "Sandy is a two-toed sloth living in the rainforest in Guyana. She meets Caio, a ten-year-old boy who lives nearby and loves two-toed sloths, right when she's been separated from her family. The two become fast friends, but danger and enemies lurk in the forest they love, and they must be careful"--Provided by publisher.
Identifiers: ISBN 9781612544250
Subjects: LCSH: Sloths--Guyana--Juvenile fiction. | Human-animal relationships--Juvenile fiction. | Rain forests--Guyana--Juvenile fiction. | CYAC: Sloths--Guyana--Fiction. | Human-animal relationships--Fiction. | Rain forests--Guyana--Fiction.
Classification: LCC PZ7.1.O873 Sa 2020 | DDC [E]--dc23

ISBN 978-1-61254-425-0
LCCN 2019909859

Printed in the United States
10 9 8 7 6 5 4 3 2 1

For more information or to contact the author, please go to
www.TheSlothSpot.com.

Dedication

To Deana, who recognized in me what I didn't recognize in myself. Your love and support have provided a lifetime of adventure and helped me accomplish the dream of a lifetime.

Acknowledgments

Thank you to those who helped create this first book about Sandy. Writing it was a dream come true. I'd like to thank my family for giving me so much encouragement to continue, Deana for her inspiration and ideas, and Kim for her example and creativity, which helped me reorganize, rethink, and rewrite; her talent and inspiration create limitless possibilities. I'd also like to thank Jen for her original thinking with the title, Annika and Bentley for their honest feedback, Dannie Ryan for her visionary illustrations, Carey Lynn Bushnell for her talented photographic gifts, and Karen Matlock, DVM, for taking such good care of Sandy.

Thanks also to Sherry LeVine and the talented folks from Brown Books Publishing Group for taking a chance on me.

The leaves gently waved under the hot breath of the camouflaged predator. His yellow eyes focused on the nearby pond in search of his next meal. He waited, motionless, searching the shrubs and shoreline for his next prey.

Patience is a virtue shared by all great hunters. Diablo was no exception.

The two-hundred-pound panther had been given his name, which meant "devil," by the people that lived near his part of the Amazon rain forest. He thought it a fitting name for the king of the jungle.

The morning was hot and humid. Diablo normally loved the smell of the hot and sticky summer days in his home near the equator, but today he was on the hunt. He was more interested in the rumbling of his stomach. It had been more than forty-eight hours since his last meal. He was determined that his hunger would end before today's sunset.

The pond was a good place to hunt. The nearby plants and bushes provided cover for his next meal. They also provided cover for Diablo. He was hidden in the shadows close to the water. Years of experience stalking his prey had taught him to keep still until the right moment presented itself.

On the actual pond, there was little shade from the late morning sun. There was little protection for any of the animals hoping to hunt, fish, or drink the fresh water of the pond.

Diablo was waiting downwind, where none of the animals that came to the pond would smell him. His plan would pay off today.

The wind gusted, and with the breeze came the smell of Diablo's next meal. His stomach ached with anticipation. He made no move to give himself away, but his heart rate sped up as he prepared to spring.

Then, he saw it: a movement in the bushes near the shoreline. *It might be the wind*, thought Diablo, but it also might be exactly what he had been waiting for. Yes, there it was again: a ripple of the leaves on the bushes.

Ten feet to the left of the rustling bush, Diablo saw the lower limb of an acai palm bobbing up and down. Diablo guessed it was an adult Amazon tapir, eating the fruit off the acai palm. He had seen many of them before. He expected the tapir's next move would be toward the pond to feed on aquatic plants. Diablo got ready for the takedown. Tapirs had short, stubby legs, but when alerted, they were capable of quick bursts of speed.

Diablo looked at the distance between his hiding place and the water's edge. The area in between had grass cover—about a foot off the ground. He would need to crawl through the grasses, crouched, to reach the kill zone. He was an expert at blending his movements with the waving grass so as not to attract the attention of his prey. The key was patience. If he moved too fast, he would fail. One wrong move could give him away.

He would not make a mistake today. With confidence, Diablo lowered his stomach to the ground and crept forward toward his unsuspecting meal.

He knew where the tapir would come out from the bushes. Unless the tapir had a buddy lookout, he would have no way of knowing what was coming. Diablo kept close to the ground as he moved—slow and steady—toward his target.

He knew to watch for other obstacles. Animals share a warning instinct. When Diablo came to hunt, the alarm could pass instantly from one animal to another. A screech from a hidden fowl or the sudden flight of an antelope in the brush could signal danger to the tapir. He would flee quickly in the opposite direction.

But now Diablo had made it to a safer area, with longer and thicker grass cover. His view of the pond was better. He knew he would see the tapir any minute. He was close. He crept a few more steps forward and stopped.

If the tapir became aware of him, Diablo's chances of eating today were much smaller. Diablo's speed in the jungle was unmatched, but if the tapir ran suddenly, it would likely escape. No—Diablo's best chance was to completely surprise his prey. He could

crush an unsuspecting animal's skull in one bite. Diablo was powerful and fast. But he had been disappointed before.

The bushes moved again. Diablo was ready for the kill. The tapir did not know he was there.

Never let your guard down in the jungle, Diablo thought to himself. In the jungle, survival required constant attention and a little bit of luck. Unfortunately for the tapir, its luck was about to run out.

The tapir sealed his fate in the next moment. Without looking around, he came to the edge of the water and reached in with his trunk-like snout to devour the aquatic plants in the pond.

This was Diablo's chance. Silently, he inched forward again, crawling toward the tapir. Diablo was almost disappointed. This kill was going to be too easy.

The tapir remained unaware. The time had come. The hunt was drawing to a close.

Time seemed to slow as Diablo leapt into the air. As the moment of impact neared, the toucans perched in the nearby tree signaled death was imminent with a long, loud screech of alarm. But no signal would save the tapir today.

Birds and animals alike rushed to escape the pond. They didn't look back at Diablo's victim.

Diablo did not let the noises of fleeing animals bother him. The tapir was his. He would eat his share and allow others to follow. Nothing was wasted in the jungle.

1 CAIO

Caio rubbed the sleep from his eyes. The morning in his house seemed dark and dreary after the dreams of the night before, but his mother had been in twice to tell him to get up and get ready for school. If Caio didn't hurry, he was going to be late for the second time this week.

Caio was ten years old. He liked school well enough, but he liked learning on his own more than he did sitting in class and listening to his schoolteacher, Mrs. Moreno. Just the night before, he had stayed up gazing at the stars, wondering how they got there.

Mrs. Moreno didn't understand. She was a short woman with a little gray in the dark hair around her temples. She usually smiled when she saw Caio, but she was also strict and rule oriented. She didn't approve of Caio's preference for hands-on learning.

Caio sighed, slid his legs off the side of the bunk bed, and sat up. He stretched his arms high and yawned. His mother's voice floated in from the kitchen. "Caio, are you up yet?"

"Yeah, yeah. I'm up, I'm up," Caio muttered.

"You better be up, mister!" his mother called back, a stern note of warning in her voice. "If you're late again, you'll be in trouble with Mrs. Moreno, and I can't help you this time!"

"Mom, I'm up! I promise!" Caio shouted, exasperated. He knew Mrs. Moreno had a tendency to scold latecomers. Caio had been on the receiving end of her lectures on more than one occasion.

Caio stood in the semidarkness of his bedroom. He was not going to be late today. He dressed quickly and bolted to the kitchen, grabbing a banana from the kitchen table as he scrambled through the front room.

He had just cleared the front door when his mother's voice stopped him. "Caio, come back here now and give me a kiss."

"Aw, Mom. I'm getting too old for this," Caio complained.

His mother caught his shoulder. "You stop that right now. You will never be too old to kiss your mother goodbye. Now give me a kiss and a hug."

Caio turned around. He shrugged and endured her breathtaking squeeze and a kiss on the cheek before she let him go, free to continue his journey to school.

Underneath his complaints, Caio's mother meant the world to him, though he wasn't always comfortable admitting it. He knew he could tell her anything, and most of the time, he told her everything. She always listened with a caring heart. Her name was Maria, but the one time his older brother, Ricardo, had called her that, she had thumped him along the backside of his head. Caio winced at the memory and grinned. She was "Mom" and would never be anything else.

Caio looked back over his shoulder at his home. His house was more of a shack, but he loved it anyway. Everything that was important to him was in that little house. He knew they didn't have many possessions, but he never felt deprived of anything. His father, mother, and brother were there, and there

was always enough to eat. He loved the cozy nights he spent with his family in their simple home.

Caio bounded up the trail, which led toward school. It was about a mile-and-a-half hike to the schoolhouse, and today he had to cover that distance in less time than usual.

He didn't like to hurry. Caio loved walking through the jungle. He made new discoveries almost every week. The jungle had its own orchestra of screeches, squawks, and growls, and it was Caio's favorite music. Today, however, he would have to run in order to get to school on time. *Oh well,* he thought as he scampered along the jungle path. *I can't be late again, but there will always be tomorrow.*

Panting, Caio tore into the schoolhouse just as Mrs. Moreno was saying good morning to the class. Caio ducked his head, hoping she wouldn't notice his late entrance. However, when Caio peeked toward his teacher, he noticed her eyes dart in his direction. She shook her head slightly. She had seen him. Without offering any excuse, Caio dropped his head, shrugged his shoulders, and headed toward his chair against the far wall.

The school was a little two-room building that stood in the middle of the Amazon rain forest. Caio's dad had led a group in building the school a few years before. Assisted by other men in the area, he had helped clear trees and jungle brush to construct the simple schoolhouse for the kids in the area.

There were two classes, one for each room of the building. The first class, taught by Mrs. Moreno, instructed kids from ages five to twelve. The second class had the older, teenage kids with Mrs. Sanchez. Caio's brother, Ricardo, was in that class. To Caio, it seemed that Ricardo always had a lot of homework. Caio had no patience for homework. It kept him from all of his exploratory adventures.

This morning, Mrs. Moreno wanted her class to improve their reading skills. "Everyone, grab a book and read for thirty minutes. When you are finished reading, write a one-paragraph summary of what you read." Mrs. Moreno looked around at her glassy-eyed class and, without expecting a response, asked, "Any questions? No? Then get started!"

Caio leapt out of his seat and bounded toward the worn bookshelf at the front of the room. He zeroed in on his favorite book about rainforest animals just as another girl reached for it. Caio snatched the book off the shelf before his classmate had it in her grasp. She looked like she wanted to protest, but Mrs. Moreno called, "Select your books and get started, please!" Caio took advantage of the opportunity to settle into his seat before his schoolmate had a chance to complain.

He cracked open the book and drank in the colorful pictures. He knew the layout well and started with the red-eyed tree frog. He was careful to avoid the section on snakes.

Caio was not a fan of snakes.

He thumbed over to the bright pages on rainforest birds to say a quick hello to his favorite bird, the Amazon toucan. *No wonder you're our national bird, Toucy!* Caio thought as he smiled to himself. He took another moment to admire the bird, then decided he wanted to take a closer look at the pages about his absolute favorite animal, the two-toed sloth.

The most noticeable feature of a sloth was how slowly the creature moved. Caio loved to run, so he couldn't comprehend always taking life at such a slow pace.

Caio fell into a daydream. He imagined climbing up a tree next to a sloth. He opened his mouth to ask the sloth a question, but found that even speaking was a long, deliberate process! He decided to watch the sloth climb instead of trying to talk to it.

He noticed the innocent, pleading eyes, the markings around the eyes, the two finger claws, and how the sloth liked hanging upside down.

Mrs. Moreno's irritated voice cut into his imaginings. "Caio Diego Santana Garcia! What are you doing?!"

Caio knew the sound of his full name meant trouble. "Uh, M-Mrs. Moreno," he stammered, embarrassed. "I was just . . ." Caio trailed off as he found himself at a loss for words.

Mrs. Moreno didn't wait for an explanation. "It is easier to read if you have your eyes open. I will not tolerate sleeping in my class."

"Yes ma'am." Caio bowed his head sheepishly. He was red, ashamed at being called out in front of his classmates. He chanced a glance around the room and saw several faces turned toward him. With the book in his lap, he lowered his forehead to the edge of the desk and gathered his arms around his head as a shield from prying eyes.

When reading time was through, Mrs. Moreno reminded the students to write their paragraph. She told them that she would choose a few lucky souls to read their work aloud. Caio was still embarrassed from earlier. He hoped she would not call on him.

Caio sighed deeply and began to feel his heart rate slow to normal when Mrs. Moreno did not call on him to participate. He listened while a few students read their paragraphs, his legs twitching with impatience.

Then, the bell! It was the sweet sound of freedom for Caio, signaling the dismissal for recess. Caio bolted out of the door. Recess was his favorite part of the day. He ran over to the open field, where his friends were already dividing into teams. The game was always the same: soccer. A few kids were rigging old fishing nets between some trees for goals. The field was open and smooth but lacked lines to show the boundaries of the game or any proper goals. This never bothered the kids. Their imaginations were more than enough to regulate these conditions.

Today, Caio was happy to find himself on the same team as his brother, Ricardo. This was excellent, as

Ricardo always set Caio up for the best chances to score. About ten minutes into their game, Ricardo passed the ball to Caio. But this time, in his eagerness to score a goal, Caio kicked wildly and sent the ball soaring over the makeshift net and into the jungle.

The other team cheered. "Ah ha! No point! Better go and get the ball, little Caio!"

Caio smiled. Their teasing was good natured and didn't bother him. He headed for the forest to retrieve the ball.

He was a few feet past the tree line when he heard a rustling noise overhead. Distracted from the task at hand, Caio whipped his head up and started scanning the trees. Was it a monkey? A toucan?

After a moment, he realized he had initially overlooked the source of the noise because it was moving at such a slow rate. It appeared to be a massive, two-headed hairball.

"Wow, you don't see that every day," whispered a voice behind him. Caio jumped and whirled around, his heart pounding.

His brother chuckled and held up his hands. “Sorry! Didn’t mean to scare you!”

“You didn’t scare me,” Caio huffed, turning back toward the trees. “What is that, anyway?”

“You don’t recognize it?” Ricardo smiled. “That, little brother, is a mother sloth carrying her new baby.”

Caio’s eyes widened in amazement. He was just a few feet from an actual sloth! The mother was moving steadily from branch to branch about halfway up a tree. Caio caught a quick glimpse of a tiny, hairy face and instantly wished he could see more. A little piece of his heart connected with the miniature sloth. He wanted nothing more than to spend all afternoon there in the forest, watching the mother and baby make their way home.

“C’mon, Caio,” Ricardo prodded, holding the ball out to him. “Let’s get back to the game before recess is over.”

“Yeah, yeah,” Caio mumbled as he turned his body to leave without turning his head away from the sloths.

Ricardo paused at the tree line to look back at his little brother. "Caio!"

Caio immediately turned on his heel and ran back out onto the field. He knew he would have a hard time focusing for the rest of the day.

Baby Sloth craned her neck to watch the two boys scamper out of the trees. They had hair only on the top of their oversized heads. She didn't understand the way they moved. They looked so strange compared to other animals she had seen in the forest.

She pulled back slightly from her mother and gestured toward the retreating figures. "Those skinny amnimals look weird."

Her mom chuckled to herself. "Those an-i-mals"—she said the word slowly, demonstrating the correct pronunciation—"are called 'humans.' They live where trees used to grow."

Baby Sloth's innocent eyes widened at such a prospect. "No trees?"

Her mother nodded again. "Yes. They live very differently from us. Humans are ground creatures.

They live in those square, flat box structures near the ground and rarely climb in the trees."

Baby Sloth glanced toward the dark earth and cuddled closer to her mom. She felt her mom's arm instinctively tighten around her. Baby Sloth had only visited the ground a few times in her life. She had climbed down the tree to go to the bathroom. Without the tree cover, she had felt exposed and vulnerable to the dangers that lurked in the forest. She shuddered at the memory of how isolated she felt at those times. She had made friends with monkeys and macaws alike, but those who dwelt on the ground did not seem as though they should always be trusted.

Her mom seemed to follow her train of thought. "We don't see a lot of humans in the forest. Some of them are dangerous, and some are friendly. You just never know with humans. Be very careful if you ever see one, and always stay in the trees."

Baby Sloth nodded her head in agreement and yawned. It was the middle of the day, and she was usually asleep. She nestled her head close to her mother and closed her eyes. She felt safe in her mother's arms. She loved that feeling of security. She could always count on her mom's presence to calm her when the outside world seemed to get too close. There was much to learn to survive in the world when everything was new.

Her mom began a slow, deliberate climb toward their home. Her methodical swinging through the branches of the trees lulled the baby sloth gently to sleep.

She awoke hours later to birds singing as the sun began to hide behind the mountains. Baby Sloth had slept through the light of the day. There was a grumbling in her midsection—her stomachs crying out for food. Baby Sloth cracked open her eyes to look at the familiar sight of her mother's face. Her mom was already wide awake. Baby Sloth glanced around to find her older brother stretching slowly from his perch high up in the tree. He liked to express his independence by sleeping higher up than where she and her mom slept. Often, he went off on his own as well.

As if on cue, her brother yawned. "Hello," he said. "Time to eat. See you later."

Baby Sloth felt her mom sigh deeply. "Hold on a minute. Let's travel to our meal together today. Do you have someplace to be?"

Her brother nodded. "Yeah, my friends and I heard about a new place over that ridge where the leaves are fresh and the bananas are sweet."

Her mom smiled bravely. Baby Sloth knew her mother understood her oldest child's need for independence, but it still hurt her sometimes. Her mother said softly, "All right, bud. You have fun with your friends, and be careful. The talk in the trees indicates there is a growing anaconda colony south of here. Don't go to the ground, and be back soon, OK ?"

He started his slow climb off of their tree as he replied, "Yeah, Mom. I'll be fine, promise. Those anacondas are more afraid of me than I am of them." Baby Sloth looked at him with admiration. He was so fearless! But when her mother looked worried, he quickly added, "But I won't go down to the ground! I'll be back. See you later!"

Baby Sloth watched her brother retreat. Then she looked at her mom. For a moment, her mom kept looking at the spot where her brother had been. She quickly brightened, however. She turned to Baby Sloth and asked, “Ready to eat?”

Baby Sloth’s multichambered stomach answered for her. It groaned with hunger. Her mom’s eyes sparkled as she laughed. “Let’s get leaves in a couple of those stomachs so they will stop growling. Then we can grab some bananas for dessert. What do you think?”

Baby Sloth grinned up at her mom. Bananas were an absolute treat. She excitedly shifted positions on her mom’s belly to get a better vantage point through the trees as they climbed.

The darkness settled around the forest as they ate. Baby Sloth heard sounds change as the daytime creatures went to sleep and her nocturnal neighbors woke. There was something more serene about starlight, accompanied by the calming sounds of the night.

Baby Sloth contentedly ate her fill in the soft moonlight. When they had finished, her mom turned to her and said, "OK ! Big night ahead of us! Time for climbing lessons!"

Baby Sloth wasn't sure how she felt about this, but she listened to her mother's instructions. Her mom took her a little lower in the trees to a long, sturdy branch. "You're going to be great," she encouraged. "We are born with a climbing instinct. You'll get the hang of it in no time."

Baby Sloth smiled bravely at her mother. She extended a shaking front claw along the tree branch, exactly as her mother had done while holding her for all of her young life. She slowly hooked her claw around the limb, bringing a back claw forward in the same manner. Methodically, she continued on. Front claw, back claw. Front claw, back claw. She stole a quick glance back at her mother and was shocked to see how much progress she had made!

Distracted, Baby Sloth missed the branch she was reaching for with her front claw. She panicked. Her back claw slipped, and the next thing she knew, she was unsupported and free-falling to the earth.

Baby Sloth let out a frightened scream and drew her claws protectively around her head. She landed, curled into a ball, in a fresh pile of leaves on the ground.

Unhurt but frightened, Baby Sloth looked around for her mother. The forest was dark. She felt vulnerable and unprotected on the ground. She had no idea how far she had fallen or where her mother was. She whimpered, eyes wide.

"Nice landing. If you have to fall, leaves are better than rocks!" Her mother's comforting voice came from up above. Baby Sloth whipped her head skyward and felt her racing heart calm as she laid eyes on her mom.

Her mother climbed down and gingerly helped the distressed baby sloth back on to the tree. "Don't worry," she murmured, soothing Baby Sloth. "Even big sloths fall sometimes. The important thing is to get back to the tree quickly." Baby Sloth latched on tightly to the front of her mother, not ready to let her go.

She felt safe in her mother's arms. Ten feet away, on the ground and out of her sight, was the farthest she had ever been from her mother. It had been so scary! Baby Sloth promised herself she would be more careful in the future.

It took a few more minutes for her mother to convince her to try again, but as time passed, she felt quite comfortable on her training branch. She enjoyed the freedom as long as she could still see her mother.

"All right, you want to climb to dinner?" her mom asked. Baby Sloth felt nervous as she surveyed her familiar branch. "Don't worry, I'll be right behind you to catch you if you slip again. Though you look so great out there climbing that, if I didn't know better, I would think you've been climbing for weeks!"

Her mother's encouragement made Baby Sloth feel more confident. Without another word, she smiled and began the short journey up the tree to the dinner area, following her mother's instructions.

They met up with her brother and ate a hearty meal of more leaves and bananas, their favorite. The three of them shared experiences from their day and enjoyed the comfort of each other's company as they

ate. As the dawn broke, it was time for bed. Baby Sloth felt a strong sense of satisfaction as she comfortably snuggled into her mother. She knew she had a lot to learn about the forest she called home, but having this safe space to return to each night made the dangers of the wider jungle seem so far away. With her family by her side, Baby Sloth felt she could take on anything that came her way.

"Caio! Caio! Wake up! It's time to go!"

Caio groaned in annoyance and then felt a sharp flicking on his ear. "Caio, if you don't get up now, Mom will be in here soon, and neither of us wants that," Ricardo told him.

Ricardo's appeal finally got through to Caio. Confused, he rubbed sleep from his eyes. He looked at his older brother standing over him. "Mom has already been in a few times," Ricardo explained. "Get up! Breakfast is ready, and she wants us in the kitchen now!"

Caio, bleary eyed and stiff, climbed down from the top bunk. He had been up quite late last night, staring at the stars through the open window near their bunk beds.

Caio loved looking up at the night sky and thinking about the cosmic heavens. It was easy to let his thoughts wander into the realm of infinite possibilities. Caio thought about being in the stars and maybe someday exploring new worlds as the first space pioneer from Guyana, South America. *What were they made of? How did they come to be? Why did the stars twinkle? What was beyond the stars?* His curiosity had kept him up well past his bedtime. Now he was feeling the consequences of his late-night daydreaming.

The rickety bunk bed squeaked as Caio pushed off of the final wooden slat and onto the floor. He slept on the top bunk while Ricardo had the bottom. His older brother had explained that it was his responsibility to protect Caio in case any forest predator made its way into their little home. Caio didn't mind. He enjoyed having easy access to the small, framed opening in the wall he called his window.

Caio dressed quickly, as he did nearly every morning, and swiftly made his way out to the kitchen.

Caio's mom greeted him. "Morning, sleepy head! Sheesh, I almost thought you needed some extra convincing this morning. Your dad has already left for the day." She turned her back to the tiny open fire stove where she was cooking fresh tortillas and eggs for her two sons.

Ricardo and Caio looked at each other. They exchanged knowing smiles. If they didn't get up promptly each morning, their mom took it upon herself to "convince" them by pulling the hair on their legs. Caio nodded a silent thank-you to his brother. Ricardo winked his reply.

"All right, Mom. I'm taking off." Ricardo stood with his empty plate and kissed his mom on the cheek. "Mrs. Sanchez is teaching an early-hour foreign language class. I want to be on time."

Maria turned and hugged her oldest son. "All right. Be safe, pay attention, and have a good day!"

Caio watched his brother leave out the front door and down the homemade wooden steps as he munched on his breakfast. He couldn't imagine voluntarily going to an early class that wasn't required. His mom had tried to explain it to him a few times. French, while not their native language, was used in other areas of the world and could help Ricardo get a better job when he was finished with school, which was sooner than Caio wanted to admit. Caio still couldn't see any good reason for sitting through another hour of school.

Caio didn't like to think about Ricardo leaving. As brothers went, Caio and Ricardo were close. Even with Ricardo's added responsibilities at school, he always found time to spend with his little brother.

Caio quietly finished his breakfast. His mother hugged and kissed him, and he was out the door in a flash. He bounded toward the schoolhouse with all of the energy his two legs could muster.

Caio smirked with satisfaction as he took his seat in the classroom. Mrs. Moreno was just standing up to greet the class. It was always a good day when he wasn't scolded for being late.

"Good morning, class. Today, we are doing our book presentations. We will go around the room one by one until everyone has had a chance to present." Caio's smirk vanished as his stomach dropped. *Book presentation?* Had he missed something? Then, from a small corner of his mind, he seemed to remember

Mrs. Moreno saying something about a presentation as he was running out of the door at the end of the day. *I thought she was talking about something else! That's not fair!*

Caio took a few deep breaths and tried to keep calm. Internally scrambling, he listened to the first few students and noticed that each presentation was on the book they had read the other day. He breathed a sigh of relief. He dreaded speaking in front of everyone, but at least he would get to talk about something he loved—the animals of the rainforest.

Caio blocked out the next few presentations as he mentally prepared a quick list of details to share. Mrs. Moreno's voice brought him out of his thoughts and back into reality. "Caio, your turn."

He swallowed, his heart pounding faster than normal as he awkwardly walked to the front of the class. "My report is about the animals in the rainforest." He tried to chase away any anxiety he felt with forced enthusiasm. "My personal favorite is Linnaeus's two-toed sloth!"

Almost immediately, he began talking quicker as his mouth tried to keep up with his thoughts. His excitement about the rainforest sloths grew with each new thought. "They are named that because they have two claws here"—he pointed to his hand—"and three claws on their back legs." He pointed to his feet. He nodded. "Yeah. Two on front"—he held up two fingers on each hand high in the air—"and three on back." He lifted his right foot in the air. "They live in the trees and climb like this." Caio demonstrated hanging upside down as best he could, on his back on the floor with his hands and feet in the air imitating a sloth climbing a tree.

He continued, "And they are *so* slow! Did you know that sometimes sloths grow algae on them because they're moving so slowly? Can you imagine! Algae growing on you because—well, anyways.

"But," he held up a finger, "that doesn't mean they can't be quick. When they defend themselves or swim, their claws come out and *slash, slash!*" He made swiping gestures with his hands through the air as he made the noises. "They can move really fast when they feel threatened. Which is good, because sloths are in danger from a lot of things. Snakes"—Caio shuddered slightly—"big birds, and jaguars!" Solemnly, Caio added, "And poachers. Poachers like to hunt sloths like they hunt everyone in the forest." He shook his head in disgust.

Caio's face brightened and his eyes sparkled as a new thought suddenly came to him. He smiled wide. "And did you know that sloths have to poop only once a week? Can you imagine—" Shocked laughter from his classmates drowned out his last question.

Mrs. Moreno suddenly rose from her chair. She moved to the front of the class. "All right, that's enough. Thank you, Caio. Very informative. You may take your seat." She cleared her throat as she glared at her students, demanding their attention.

Caio breathed a deep sigh of relief. It was over! He honestly couldn't remember what the other book reports covered, but he blankly watched with a big smile plastered on his face for the rest of the period.

As soon as they were dismissed for lunch, Caio burst out of the tiny room and onto the open field.

Everyone who wanted to play soccer divided up into teams. Caio and Ricardo were on opposite teams today. They ran around the field, practicing their footwork as they passed the ball back and forth while looking for an opening to score.

Ricardo was an excellent soccer player, but his desire for Caio to succeed overcame his competitive nature when he played against his younger brother's team. Caio took full advantage of his brother's hesitation and gained control of the ball, dribbling down the field. He thought he even saw Ricardo push a member of his own team when they were about to steal the ball from Caio. Ricardo's teammate tripped and tried to regain his footing as Caio, beaming, sent the ball flying into the goal.

"Gooooooaaaaal!" Ricardo scooped up his little brother as he shouted the announcement for the entire forest to hear.

Caio laughed and threw his hands in the air, celebrating. Ricardo lowered him to the ground right in front of the goal to receive the congratulations of his teammates.

While Caio enjoyed the recognition from his teammates, he stopped and cocked his head to one side. The goal was directly in front of the lush forest he had often explored. Even at this time of celebration, his thoughts turned to the other day, when he and Ricardo had seen the mother sloth carrying her baby. Were they in there today? Were they safe? Would he get to see them again?

"Caio, Caio! Nice goal, dude, but the game goes on," the goalie called. "Hurry, get out on the field, man!"

Caio smiled to himself as he considered his last thought. *Yes*, he thought to himself, *I think I will find those sloths again!*

5
DIABLO

Diablo strolled through the trees, surveying his kingdom. The panther was full and content after a recent chase and meal. He felt the respect of the entire jungle for his role as king of the rainforest. He admired the sights and smells of the forest as he prowled through the leafy trees.

The damp earth sloped upward as Diablo wandered into a clearing of trees. He took note of each tree he passed by. Memories flooded his mind. The top of this clearing marked the spot where Diablo had made his first kill. He remembered when he had had a family and his father had taught him how to hunt.

Those were good times, he thought to himself.

But in this place of good memories, there was an unfamiliar smell. Diablo tensed. He bent low to the ground. His belly brushed the dirt.

The new smell left Diablo uncertain. He shook his head, trying to clear the scent. Something wasn't right.

Diablo stretched his paws. If he were to investigate, he would need to do so in complete silence. He inched forward, focused on the new, foul smell.

The scent grew sour as he stalked forward. His ears caught faint, deep voices in the wind. But when he saw the source of the scent, he instantly recognized the reason for his concern. Humans.

His experience had taught him that humans only wanted to take from the forest. They were disruptive and destructive toward his home. Humans were the reason Diablo no longer had a family. Flashing back to worse memories from his life as a cub filled Diablo with anxiety and anger. A low growl escaped his throat.

His eyes narrowed. His neck muscles flexed. He was no longer a clumsy cub. Today, he would teach these humans a lesson.

He jumped from behind the brush, coming face to face with three dirty men. Two were bent over wooden structures they were piecing together. A few finished products lay on the ground around them. Diablo recognized them from his younger days. Traps. Awful, terrible traps. They attracted and captured rainforest animals. They were tools of death and destruction, dirty tricks of weak, cowardly, and greedy hunters.

The third human, clearly their leader, stood above the other two. He had ugly features and menacing eyes, but when he saw Diablo, he froze, and his voice caught in his throat.

So weak he cannot even bark out orders, thought Diablo.

One of the others dropped his half-constructed trap on the ground in surprise. With intimidating posture, Diablo looked over the men. He could smell their fear. *Good*, he thought. He had won the mental battle with these cowards.

He leapt down and roared. The humans abandoned their project and fled.

As Diablo watched them run, he felt some small satisfaction. The humans were the helpless ones today. He considered the traps that lay on the ground.

Wooden poles had been crudely tied into a type of box, held together by lengths of strong twine. There were different sizes, and as he looked over the landscape, he noticed a few in the trees as well as on the ground.

It was just such a box that had stolen his brother. Diablo's heart screamed as he recalled a memory he had locked away. He had been a small cub, terrified. It was the only time in his life he had been so overcome by fear. His brother had clawed and snapped inside one of these wooden boxes, panicked and growling as he tried to escape.

Diablo had swiped and bitten at the bindings holding the wooden poles together. He had not been successful. He had been too small. He remembered the sour stench of the humans growing closer. He had tried to attack them but had been kicked aside into a tree with such force he had lost consciousness. Leaving him for dead, the two-legged demons had left him without a brother. He had never seen his brother again.

It had been the worst day of his life, but Diablo was not so small now. With one swipe of his massive paws, he destroyed the wooden box in front of him. If only he could have set his brother free in the same way. Diablo tilted his head in the direction of the retreating humans. Never again would they invade his home.

His muscles tight, he exploded into a powerful run after the men. He spotted them in the distance, shouting to each other as they ran toward a strange red device with four round wheels holding it off the ground. Diablo recognized the machine as their escape and sprinted toward them. He was faster than anything or anyone in the jungle, including these intruders. He wanted to catch them before they reached the safety of their machine. They had to pay for their crimes against the jungle and his family.

Gaining ground on the men, Diablo felt only grim satisfaction. He would protect the forest with everything he had. He could hear the frightened yells of the humans and smell the stench of fear on them, overpowering everything else about them now. He was close.

But not close enough. The men had reached their machine. It growled to life as one man climbed into the front. The back was an open bed of metal. A second man dived into it headfirst. Only one man was left on foot as Diablo closed in on them.

The machine jerked forward as the humans sought to escape the angry black panther. The two men already safe were selfish enough to try and leave their companion behind. The last man desperately hurled himself forward just as Diablo leapt into the air, snapping at his heels. The human barely made it into the back of the machine, shouting frantically to the man in the front. The machine roared loudly as it gained speed, crashing through several wooden contraptions on its way out of Diablo's reach and out of the forest.

Diablo halted in his tracks and snorted. He was unhappy the humans had escaped, but there was no point in continuing to chase them now. He had made his point. He would exercise no mercy if they returned to his forest.

With a powerful grace and dignity, Diablo returned to the clearing and destroyed each of the wooden traps with a satisfying swipe.

He was the only one allowed to hunt in this forest. His forest. He understood the circle of life. It could be cruel to those lower on the food chain, but it was fair. As rulers of the jungle went, he was a reasonable one. He only hunted when he needed to eat, in the time-honored tradition of the forest. Humans preyed on weak and helpless animals for their own gain, not for survival.

If Diablo had no family, he had a duty. He protected the forest. If an animal served his needs every couple of days, it was no more than his due. The humans were abusive, wasteful, and excessive in their hunt. They, too, would get what they deserved, should they ever return.

Diablo looked out in the direction of the retreating humans. "Never come here again," he said. "This is my home."

6
CAIO

Caio woke to silence. It was Saturday, which meant no school. A huge grin spread over his face. He flung back his sheet, threw his legs over the side of the battered bunk bed, and jumped down with an excitement he never had this early on a school day. It was funny that Caio, during the week, would hope and pray for extra time in bed each morning. Waking up for school was pure torture. Today, his parents would let him sleep if he chose to, but he was wide awake in the stillness of the morning, looking forward to adventure.

The unsteady bunk bed swayed slightly as he landed, and Ricardo let out a sleepy moan. "Caio, brother, what in the world are you doing? Go back to bed."

Thoroughly unconvinced, Caio smirked as he got dressed. *Not today, Ricardo!* Caio thought.

The sun was just peeking over the horizon, a dusty light creeping its way into their little home. Caio poked his head out of his room just in time to see his mother come out from her room, still rubbing sleep from her eyes.

She smiled when she saw her youngest son. "Caio. You're awake. What's going on with you today?" She cocked her head slightly.

"I'm going exploring, Mom!" Caio blurted.

And maybe I can even find the baby sloth again! he thought.

Maria knew all about her son's love for the outdoors. She nodded her head. "All right. Make sure you eat before you go out today, OK ?"

"On it!" Caio ran out of his bedroom and into the kitchen. Within a few minutes he had eaten a small breakfast, washed it down with homemade nectar juice, and bounded out the front door.

The soft sunlight seemed to hum along with Caio as he skipped down the path that took him to the forest. The path dipped slightly downward then back up as Caio picked up his pace. He knew if he could get his momentum just right, he would be able to jump on top of a large, moss-covered boulder just ahead.

Bunching up his muscles, Caio leapt. He landed perfectly, spun around, and jumped back down again, not a care in the world to weigh him down.

Off to the side of this well-known path was a small pond. A twisted tree branch bent low over the top of the water. Caio jumped again, taking hold of the branch and swinging right to the opposite edge of the pond. He stopped for a minute to observe the green vegetation growing through the water near the bank.

Movement off to the left caught his eye. Caio bent down to take a closer look. He was sure something small had hopped into the water. It didn't take him long to find it. As he watched, something in the water turned a brilliant shade of neon green.

Caio reached a steady hand into the pond and picked up a red-eyed tree frog. The frog, frightened now that his initial camouflage hadn't fooled the intruder, bulged his eyes to several times larger than his eye sockets. *An ugly defense,* Caio giggled to himself. He loved it when frogs did this!

The frog's feet ballooned out. He adjusted the coloring of his sides to a bright blue and yellow.

Caio admired the display. His mouth gaped open as he watched the nonpoisonous frog changing colors right in front of him. His hand loosened slightly.

The frog took his chance to escape. He hopped out of Caio's cupped hand, furiously pumping his legs. He fell back to the pond and swam to a nearby log, disappearing behind the water-worn wood.

Caio was not disappointed. He did not want to keep the frog, and the tiny amphibian had never been in danger from him. He clapped his hands together as he looked all around, deciding where to go from here. Caio splashed out of the pond and back onto the main path into the forest.

As he approached the tree line, Caio stopped to observe his surroundings. He had been in this forest hundreds of times. His father had made certain to teach him to be careful when he explored. For as young as he was, he was remarkably wise to the ways of the jungle. He felt comfortable in the dense, humid tree cover.

The music of the jungle Caio so loved grew louder as he walked deeper into the forest. Chattering monkeys and birds were up above, while the croaking of frogs and insects added to the mix. If he paused and concentrated hard enough, he could even hear the *drip, drip, drip* of water falling from the uppermost leaves toward the ground.

He was surrounded by every shade of green imaginable as he picked his way along the damp forest path. The dense forest eventually gave way to a clearing in the trees where streaks of sunlight peeked through the leaves. Caio squinted his eyes, his skin warmed by the sudden appearance of the sun.

He directed his gaze forward on the trail and caught a glimpse of a rainbow! Caio smiled as he moved toward the colorful display, but his smile faded as he noticed something strange. *That's odd,* Caio thought to himself. *This rainbow is all orange colored.* A foreboding feeling stopped Caio dead in his tracks. Had the rainbow just moved? *No,* he decided. It was just flickering in the humidity. *Right?*

His eyes widened. He'd definitely seen the rainbow moving! His heart began to thump loudly in his chest. The orange-tinted rainbow was headed directly for him!

Caio remembered his rainforest book at school and suddenly wished he hadn't skipped over the section about snakes. He gulped. He hated snakes. But he was fairly positive that the fake rainbow in front of him was actually a Brazilian rainbow boa. Even though Caio felt calmer knowing that this particular snake wasn't poisonous, he had no desire to come face to face with it.

Caio kept his eyes on the snake's movements as he carefully shifted toward a nearby tree stump. Carefully and methodically, Caio made his way around the back of the stump and ducked behind it. He took a deep breath as he rested the back of his head against the wood for a moment. Sweat ran down his forehead.

Circumstances could change so quickly in the forest.

He knew that he was not in any real danger. Still, he felt safer behind the tree stump. After a moment, he watched the snake slither past.

He guessed this rainbow boa was about seven feet long. Its orange-tinted skin reflected the sun's rays in its unique rainbow pattern. Looking more closely, Caio noticed the scaly body was covered in half-moon designs. The snake let out a low hiss when it saw him. Caio's uneasiness quickly returned. He watched the snake slither away and slowly edged his body in the opposite direction. He began walking forward, letting his feet take him away. He didn't pay attention to where he was going, looking back over his shoulder until he was certain the snake was gone.

In a few more minutes, Caio began looking forward again. But still nervous, every couple of moments, he looked back over his shoulder to make sure the snake was still headed in the opposite direction.

Crack! Caio ran into something solid. The force of the blow was enough to knock him backward to the ground. Dazed, sitting on the damp earth, Caio reached up to rub a quickly rising bump that was forming on the side of his head. He squinted, looking at the object he'd hit.

It was a tree. Caio, in his determination to keep an eye on the snake, had run smack into a tree. He laughed out loud. He got to his feet and continued to rub the soreness on his head.

Caio looked around. He knew where he was. He sighed, deciding that his adventuring was over for today. The sloth would have to wait until his next outing. He spent his walk home rubbing his bruised head and making up stories to tell Ricardo about the snake encounter. He would never hear the end of this from his brother.

Just goes to show, Caio thought to himself, *you never know what might happen in the forest!*

7
SANDY

Jagged streaks of lightning slashed across the threatening sky. Each was followed by a loud crack of thunder. Large raindrops fell thick and hard on everything in the rainforest.

It was the beginning of the winter rain season.

Baby Sloth clung tightly to her mother's chest. This climb home was so exciting. How the tree swayed with the wind blasting through the leaves! Baby Sloth shut her eyes and buried her head in her mother's fur. She focused on her mother's movements, still slow and steady even in the middle of the thundering rainstorm. Baby Sloth felt reassured by the calm, methodical way her mother climbed despite the threatening weather. Her mother's claws never slipped or faltered, and soon they were nestled under a particularly dense patch of leaves in the cecropia tree they called home.

The rain continued relentlessly for the next few hours. Baby Sloth cuddled into her mother for comfort. As the rain slowed, her brother made his way into the tree. With the noises of the storm softening and her family around her, Baby Sloth felt safe enough to poke her head out and look at her surroundings.

Drops of water slid steadily down the leaves on the trees to the muddy earth. A nearby river was swollen with the storm. Baby Sloth could see no other animals nearby. Everyone had hidden to avoid the downpour.

Curious, Baby Sloth began to move off of her mother in the direction of the swollen river. There were a few hours left before the sun rose. Baby Sloth intended to make the most of the rest of the time she had before bed.

"And where are you off to?" her mother asked, amused.

"The river! Swimming is so much fun. And I'm really good at it!" Baby Sloth's independence was growing every day. She hoped reminding her mother of her swimming talents would get her the go-ahead to explore.

"All sloths are great swimmers, my dear," came her mother's reply. "Stay here for tonight. You never know what sort of creatures come upriver during a storm. We'll go down to the river together once the waters go back to normal, OK ?"

Baby Sloth frowned. Waiting for bedtime in the tree didn't sound like fun. But she knew her mother was right. Tales of massive anacondas and alligators patrolling rivers after a storm suddenly seemed too real. Baby Sloth shuddered at the danger in the jungle. Perhaps she could wait until the river was back to normal size.

She spent the last few hours before dawn in a relaxed silence. Mother, daughter, and son enjoyed the familiar comfort of being home as a family. They slowly drifted off to sleep under an overcast dawn.

A few hours later, a kingly macaw landed on top of the cecropia tree. His perch dipped beneath him, and a ray of sunlight fell across Baby Sloth's face. Baby Sloth cracked one eye open and moaned softly. She didn't want to get up! The macaw let out an ear-splitting

squawk and took off into the distance. But Mother Sloth passed her hand gently over Baby Sloth's face, silently urging her to sleep again. Confident her mother was still beside her, alert and awake, Baby Sloth relaxed.

Baby Sloth was drifting back to sleep when there was a rustling in the distance. She was too far gone to consider the dangers, but she heard, as if in a dream, her brother's and mother's voices.

"Where are you going, Mom? Did you hear that noise?"

"I'm going down there to go to the bathroom. I was just going to sneak down while you and your sister were sleeping."

"You shouldn't be going down there alone. It could be a little dangerous after the storm."

"How about we go together? That way we can keep an eye out for any unwanted visitors."

Baby Sloth heard her brother's voice, fading away. "What about her?"

"She'll be fine while we go down. Let's go."

"All right, Mom. Stay behind me. I'll go down first."

Baby Sloth shifted on her branch and slipped deeper into sleep, without paying much attention to what she heard. Her family was around her. What could possibly be wrong?

8 DIABLO

Diablo was in a foul mood. The rain had forced him to change his hunting patterns, and hunger gnawed at his stomach. It had been three days since he last ate. His instincts were still sharp, but he could feel his mind beginning to cloud with hunger.

Hunger and a lack of sleep. The storm had disturbed his rest, and when he woke, he saw that the normally smooth forest floor had become sticky with mud. The mud would slow the blinding speed he relied on to catch his prey by surprise. On the other hand, his prey would be slowed as well. In the end, it all was in balance, which was just as well. Diablo enjoyed the challenge of hunting, the thrill of testing his skills against his prey.

Thunder clapped in the distance. The storm had moved on to another area further away. He growled. He didn't like the lack of control he felt during this season of pouring rains. He was the king in this rainforest, but the storms were a reminder that there were powers even higher than him, and there was a certain beauty to nature's hierarchy.

Up above, he could hear birds lightly chattering. Diablo cursed his bad luck. Birds were the gossip line of the forest. They were no doubt warning every creature of his presence. Hunting in his usual grounds would be out of the question.

There was no point in waiting around. Diablo quickly made his way east, heading toward another hunting ground he had enjoyed as a younger adult. It had been a long time since he had been to that area of the forest. With any luck, the tree-dwelling animals wouldn't think to look for him or send out warnings. His stomach grumbled in protest as he sloshed his way through the mud.

He reached the patch of forest he desired. He slowed, testing the ground with his pads. Here, the ground was still wet, but not as treacherous as the muddy ground earlier. Maybe in this new environment, his luck would improve.

Diablo picked his way through the brush, making sure not to be spotted. His eyes darted around, taking in the layout of this part of the rainforest.

Suddenly, there was movement in his peripheral vision. As he turned to get a better view, it stopped. Had he seen something? Or was it just shadows?

He changed direction and maneuvered toward a shadowy cecropia tree. He had perfected his stealthy approach years before. Again, he saw a movement. Diablo peered through the gloom of the forest floor, and this time, his keen eyesight picked up the figures moving toward the ground. *There, on the tree: sloths, two of them,* he thought to himself. His eyes narrowed as Diablo gathered his back legs beneath him. *This might not be such a bad day after all.*

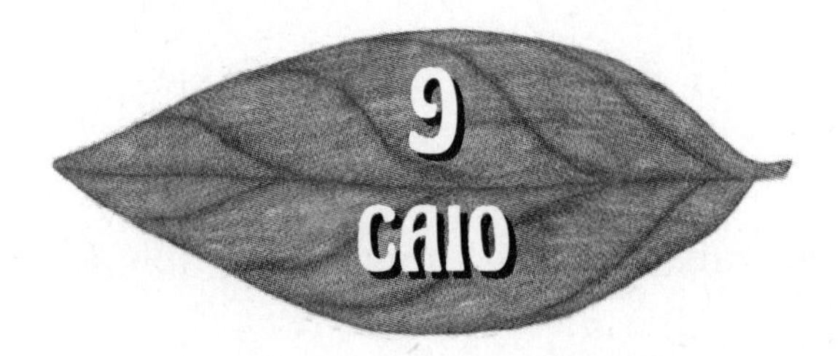

9 CAIO

Caio glanced at the small, battery-operated clock on the wall and sighed. School could not end soon enough today.

There had been gloomy rain clouds in the sky all week. Caio and his classmates had been forced to stay indoors. Caio felt like the walls were closing in around him! After a week of sitting still, he wanted to run and feel the wind in his hair. He wouldn't mind the rain as long as he could enjoy being outside. A muddy soccer field was much better than being stuck inside the small schoolroom.

The hands on the clock seemed to crawl, moving so slowly Caio could hardly stand it. Finally, Mrs. Moreno wrapped up her lesson and released her class. Many of the children looked out at the storm grimly, lingering in the doorway to avoid having to go out in the rain. But Caio ran forward and broke through the line of his classmates, practically skipping out of the schoolhouse. He threw out his hands and raised his face toward the sky. *Finally*, he thought, *I'm free!*

Caio had no interest in hurrying home. He would only be stuck inside again. Instead, he decided to stroll down the path home and explore some of the forest. The falling rain turned to sprinkles as he entered the shelter of the tree line.

The monkeys and birds above him chattered through the *drip, drip, drip* of the raindrops. Caio raised his head, catching glimpses of the light faces and dark mouths of the squirrel monkeys as they swung in and out of view. The tropical birds flying from branch to branch were streaks of bright color through the green of the canopy.

The entire scene was a work of art, and Caio was in awe of the beauty of nature around him.

Surrounded by the trees and jungle creatures, Caio felt right at home. He spotted several cecropia trees nearby, their large leaves spread like an umbrella with small, white flowers sprouting at the ends.

On the trunk of one of the trees, Caio saw a strange-looking lump. At first, he thought it was a bunch of moss. Then the lump started inching its way around the trunk of the tree. Rubbing his eyes, Caio tilted his head to one side. He squinted, trying to get a closer look.

It was a sloth, Caio realized—his favorite rainforest animal. She was hanging by her feet just beyond the point where the monkeys carried on their chattering conversation. Caio began moving toward her. He did his best to keep his movements measured and calm. He didn't want to scare her away.

She was looking right at him, he saw. Was he imagining it, or was she reaching out a greeting to him? He watched in amazement as she slowly came down from branch to branch. She seemed nervous, he thought. He decided to help ease her along.

"It's all right, *pequeño*," he promised her, using a local endearment meaning "little one." "Come on down."

Caio had an idea. Quickly, he removed the pack from his shoulder and reached inside. He glanced up and saw that the sloth had stopped in her tracks, unsure what his movements meant.

"I've got something for you," he said in soothing tones. "Here!" He took his hand out of his pack and offered her what was left from his lunch: a banana.

The sloth's eyes lit up. She began climbing down again. Caio beamed at her and peeled open the banana. He broke off a piece and held it out for her to see.

She wasn't nervous anymore. She reached her clawed hand out toward Caio's gift and pulled it toward her mouth. She smacked her lips appreciatively as she munched on the tasty fruit.

Caio fed the banana to his new friend, piece by piece. As he gave her the banana, he looked into her eyes. They were a rich, dark brown color—the kindest eyes he had ever seen.

What should I call her? he wondered. He looked her up and down, trying to find a clue. Her hair was light brown, speckled with darker brown around her face. The hair around her snout turned steadily

darker until it blended with her black nose. The different shades of brown on her fur reminded him of a familiar setting.

"I've got it!" he said, excited. "I'll call you Sandy! Like the sand at the beach!"

The sloth chewed contentedly on the banana. Caio decided she was happy with her new name.

As Sandy finished her treat, Caio began to talk to her about everything in his life. He shared with her his love for soccer and his dream to play with the Guyana national team someday. He told her about Mrs. Moreno and the trouble he often found himself in at school. He told her about his family: how his father had taught him about the forest and how his mom always had his back and how his brother was his best friend.

At the mention of his family, Caio was struck by a sudden thought. Just a few weeks ago, not too far from here, he and Ricardo had seen a mother sloth with her baby. Could this be the same sloth baby he had seen that day? If this was her, where was her mother?

"Do you have a family, little Sandy?" Caio asked softly, glancing around and hoping to catch a glimpse of another sloth. There were none.

He turned back and looked at Sandy's inviting and kind eyes. Did he imagine the sadness he now saw there?

"It's OK , Sandy. I'll always be there for you," Caio told her, reaching his hand forward. He paused right under her head, waiting to see Sandy's response. When she did not back away, Caio softly stroked the top of her head. He continued to talk to her, promising more bananas at their next meeting.

The rain let up, and Caio stayed in the forest with Sandy until the light above started to fade. He knew that if he stayed any longer, he would be late for dinner, and that would upset his mom.

He looked into Sandy's eyes. "I have to go home now," he whispered, "but I'll come back soon. I promise!" He stroked her fur one last time. "Stay safe, little Sandy."

He took a deep breath and began walking toward the path that would take him home. He turned around after a couple of steps to wave at his new jungle friend and watch her climb back up the tree.

When he was sure she was safely up the tree, Caio turned around and started skipping home. What an amazing day! He had made friends with a sloth! He knew no one would believe him, but he didn't care.

But just then, Ricardo stepped out from behind a tree on the path. Caio gasped and nearly jumped out of his skin. "Caio! What in the world was that?!" Ricardo demanded, looking back at the cecropia trees.

"Ricardo!" Caio exclaimed. "Wha—how—what are you doing here?" he stammered.

Ricardo laughed. "You were gone for a long time, and you didn't show up for our soccer game today. I figured you came to the forest. I had no idea you were such a sloth whisperer!" Ricardo punched him on the arm to congratulate him. "How long have you been friends with that sloth?" Ricardo asked excitedly.

"Just today," Caio said. He smiled, and any annoyance he felt at being scared faded as he thought of Sandy.

Ricardo looked at him with disbelief. He stopped walking. "Caio," he said seriously, "I have never seen anything like that. Ever." He spoke slowly, eyes wide. "You have a real gift, brother."

Caio felt his heart swell inside of him. He beamed back at his brother. "And I have a new friend!" Caio laughed and immediately launched into an in-depth explanation of his encounter. The sun poked through the clouds and set gently behind them as they walked down the jungle path toward home.

With the rain gone, the sun filtered through the canopy. It was a beautiful day in the rainforest. It was a big change from the rainstorms that had plagued the forest during the past few weeks. It had been such a gloomy and depressing time for Sandy. But today there was a change in the air. Birds were flying across a bright blue sky. Toucans squawked with delight at the brightness of the day.

The sun warmed the ground and dried the rain from the leaves. Sandy sat quietly and watched as a mother monkey nearby fed her new infant. Other members of the monkey troop were close, ready to protect the new mother and her young son. Sandy felt sad watching the baby monkey. Such a short time ago, she had felt just as safe in her own mother's arms.

Being alone was hard. Sandy thought back to the last day she had had a family. That last night, they had talked and laughed together as a thunderstorm moved off to the east. It had been easy to fall asleep that day. With the fresh-air smell from the rain, her mother and brother close by, and a full stomach, she had fallen asleep well before the sun rose.

When she finally woke, neither her mother nor her brother was anywhere to be found. She had searched calmly at first and then more frantically in each of the tree's top limbs. Fear had paralyzed her when she had realized that her mother and brother were gone without a trace. Whether they had gone to snack on a few more leaves or down the tree to use the bathroom, they had not returned. By sunrise the next day, Sandy had known something was terribly wrong. Her mother and brother would never abandon her. Grief had flooded her heart as she had realized she was alone, with no one in the jungle to watch over her. How could she go on without her mother and brother?

She had been too upset to eat for many days as she tried to deal with her life being turned upside down.

But eventually she had realized she had to eat, or she would become too weak to climb.

She had forced herself to eat enough to stay alive, but she had little hope of moving on. She missed her family too much. Life seemed so cruel and unfair. How did everything that had seemed so right suddenly now seem so wrong?

After a while, she had made her way back to her family's eating spot. Somehow, she had hoped she could still find her mother and brother there—but at the same time, she had known it was just a wish. The jungle was a dangerous place.

It was difficult to eat leaves when she didn't feel hungry. Some of the other mother sloths had tried to comfort her, but she hadn't wanted to listen. She wanted *her* mother.

Watching the newborn monkey now, however, Sandy was reminded of her mother in a good way. She was not jealous, she decided. She was happy for the baby monkey and was comforted to see him with his own family.

There were still good things around her. She thought of the human who had given her a banana a few days ago and spent several hours with her talking softly to her in his nonsense language. Instead of being sad and thinking about the shock of losing her family, she would focus on the good memories of her time with them. She would feel happy again. She was still very young and wanted to make her mother proud.

Sandy watched as the baby monkey fell asleep in his mother's arms. She enjoyed family life. Maybe someday she would be part of another family. Until then, she would survive and find happiness in her memories.

Today, Sandy felt like exploring. She crawled up into a different tree to take a new look at her surroundings. She normally slept during the day, but now that the rain had stopped and she was feeling a bit better, she thought it would be exciting to climb around in the daylight. But without her mother close, she would be careful.

As she climbed from limb to limb and tree to tree, she found most of her fellow rainforest animals wanted the same things she did. Friends, food, and fun were at the top of the list, but what drove every creature every minute of every day was survival. Finding enough food for each member of their family, protection from harsh weather, and staying out of the path of the many jungle predators. Although Sandy enjoyed the day's exploring, she was always careful of the unseen dangers.

By late morning, she was growing too sleepy to continue and decided she would return to her home tree for sleep. But as she turned around to climb back, she noticed something unusual on a lower limb. She did not recognize it, and Sandy felt she should be cautious. But today was a day for adventure, and so Sandy decided she would check it out.

After watching the object for several moments, during which it did not move, Sandy allowed herself to climb down to look at it more closely. It smelled and felt like bamboo, she realized, tied together in the shape of a box. But she could see through the box at any angle, and inside, there was a lovely smell.

Sandy pulled her head away as she heard another noise from below her. She dropped her front claws off the branch for a closer look. She saw a few humans—older than the boy she had met a few days ago. They were walking toward a metal object. They grunted to one another, but she couldn't understand them any more than she had understood the boy. They climbed into the metal contraption, which made a belching noise and began to slowly move away. Sandy watched it for a moment, then returned her attention to the bamboo box.

Shoots of bamboo were tied in crisscross directions. A single shoot hung down in the middle, and the smell—it was a banana in the center of the box. She was hungry, and around the other side of the box, she saw a wide opening where she could crawl inside and enjoy a snack before heading back to sleep.

As she began to move around to the open side, she wondered why she had never seen crates like this with bananas hanging in the middle. *Is this too good to be true?* she thought. The opening in the side was just big enough for her to fit, but as Sandy started to climb into the opening, a bad feeling came over her. She pulled back and thought, *This seems wrong.*

Hanging from a nearby branch, Sandy decided to take a closer look at the box. She leaned in closer. Along with the sweet scent of the banana was another unfamiliar smell. Sandy pulled back and looked off into the distance. She wondered if the smell had come from the humans, still moving away from the area. She looked around and noticed two other boxes just like the one in front of her. *I wonder if these things are dangerous,* she thought.

Sandy decided to trust her instincts and backed away from the bamboo device. Now she could see that the banana was tied to a hidden door inside the box. If she were to pull the banana toward her, the hidden door would slide down over the opening and would lock into place, trapping her inside. Sandy backed away, angry now. What she had thought was a tasty treat was just a clever trap.

She crawled on top of the box and chewed the twine holding the extra door in place. The hidden door slid away from the rest of the box and fell harmlessly to the ground. As she watched the door crash into pieces, she wondered what might have happened if she had entered the box and eaten the banana.

She could still hear the humans' strange metal nest moving away in the distance. Were they responsible for the traps in the tree? She didn't understand. The boy she had met a few days ago had fed her, too, but there had been no trap. She had felt completely safe when she was with him.

Sandy decided she would be extra careful around humans until she could determine whether they could be trusted or not.

The sun shone through the raggedy curtain over the window. Caio smiled and threw back the sheet that covered his bed. It was a beautiful day outside. He could hear the birds singing in the distance. Today was Saturday. It seemed as if the entire world celebrated with him.

He hopped down from the top bunk and dressed quickly. Usually, on Saturdays, Caio played soccer with his friends, but today he only had one thing on his mind: *Sandy*. Caio hadn't been able to think of anything else since he had met the sloth in the forest a few days ago. He wanted to find his new friend again and spend the day with her.

As Caio swung out of his room, he swiped a banana from the kitchen table. He remembered that he had promised to bring Sandy more yummy treats.

His mother's firm voice stopped him in his tracks. "Excuse me, where do you think you're going? And without breakfast?"

He turned. He felt a little guilty. In the excitement of the other day, he had not told his mom about meeting Sandy. He sighed. He didn't want to waste any sunlight. Caio decided he wouldn't tell her about Sandy just yet. It would take too much time to bring his mother up to speed. "Soccer, Mom!" Caio replied. "Got to run!" She smiled with understanding, and he bolted out of the door. The sun rose into the sky as Caio headed quickly down the familiar path into the forest. He felt like singing with the toucans and floating in the air with the butterflies. *Where is Sandy today?* he wondered. He hoped it would be easy to find her among the trees.

Thwack!

Jumping at the loud, unnatural sound, Caio hit the ground. Crouched down, he took cover behind a leafy bush. His heart pounded. His breath was short. *What was that?* He closed his eyes, listening as his father had taught him. Past the sounds of monkeys chattering in the distance, he heard it again—a sound that didn't belong in the forest. An anxious feeling began to fill his gut.

He couldn't see anything from his hiding spot. He knew he would have to move, so he took a few deep breaths to calm himself. His first concern was for Sandy. Whatever was wrong in the forest today, he hoped she was nowhere around.

Caio took inventory of his situation. He was unarmed. He had no idea what was out there. The sounds had gone now—had they been his imagination, or was there really something scary in the forest?

Thwack!

As if on cue, another heavy, dull sound echoed through the trees. Caio made up his mind: he had to investigate.

The monkeys continued to chatter as Caio inched out from behind the bush. He looked around, making sure he was alone. When he was sure there wasn't any immediate danger, he crept forward toward the place where he had heard the noise. As he got closer to its source, he began to hear other low, rumbling sounds.

His eyes narrowed in concentration as he tried his best to focus on the sounds ahead of him while making as little noise as possible.

Thwack! Thwack! Thwack!

Caio dove behind the trunk of a tree. He was close now; he could feel it. From his earlier visits into the forest, he knew there would be a clearing with trees up ahead. He shut his eyes tight and listened as hard as he could.

He was close enough now to make out the low, rumbling noises he had heard—voices! By the sounds of it, there were several gruff-sounding men up ahead, and the dull, echoing sounds were coming from the same direction. Caio took a deep breath and crawled forward.

The scene in the clearing was chaotic. Dirty men yelled back and forth as they worked. Caio saw a man add a wheelbarrow of dirt to a large mound and climb back into a hole in the earth. He tilted his head. What did it all mean? There was a rusty old red truck parked in the back of the clearing. A large sheet was draped over the contents of the truck's bed.

Thwack!

Caio snapped his head around. There it was! A man with a whip coiled on his hip and a machete in his right hand was whacking away at a low-hanging tree branch. The tree shook violently, but the branch remained partially attached to the tree. The man wound his arm back and delivered a final, forceful blow.

The tree branch fell to the ground. Attached to the falling limb was a tiny monkey. As the man picked up the monkey, the small creature shrieked. It tried to escape, but another man quickly covered it with a net and scooped it up. He placed the struggling monkey in a crudely made wooden box and tossed the box into the back of the truck.

Caio sat in stunned silence. He was frozen, staring at the horrible sight. The other monkeys in the trees around, in their own traps, screeched, helpless to escape. Tears stung Caio's eyes.

These evil men were poachers. They prowled the forest and kidnapped helpless animals. Caio wasn't exactly sure what happened to the animals once the men hauled them out of the forest, but he knew it was nothing good. His dad had often told him that poachers were not to be trusted.

Caio's fear quickly turned into anger. As small as he was, he could do nothing against the men. However, he was quick and had learned how to move quietly. There had to be a way he could use that.

Caio stepped back into the tree line and crept around the truck. He paused as the men finished their digging and covered the gaping hole with large leaves and debris. When they finished, the hole was perfectly disguised as regular ground. Caio understood. This hole was another trap set by the poachers to capture larger animals. The men clapped the dirt off of their hands and made their way to the other side of the clearing toward the man with the whip and machete. He counted quickly, taking note that there were five men in total.

This was his chance, but it wouldn't last for long. Caio leapt forward into action. He dragged the leaves off of the hole, uncovering the disguised pit. Without pausing to admire his work, Caio ran over to the rusted truck and quietly snuck into the back. He could hear the men speaking loudly and laughing as they worked. Each laugh pierced his heart. Caio set his jaw. The poachers were not going to get away with any of this today—not if he had anything to say about it.

He carefully lifted the sheet. Several pairs of sad eyes stared back at him. The cage closest to Caio housed the monkey that had just been captured. Caio glanced over to the men and mentally counted. With all five poachers accounted for, Caio set to work. He unlatched cage after cage, freeing monkeys and birds into the back of the clearing. Caio worked furiously. The noises the escaping animals were making would draw attention.

His fears were confirmed when he heard one of the men across the clearing. "Hey, didn't we just capture that monkey?"

"Did you latch the cage? Those little freaks can get out if you don't do it right. Go check it out," came the reply.

Caio panicked. He had mere moments before he was discovered. There was only one cage remaining, underneath some equipment. Caio's heart fell as he saw the animal inside the cage.

It was a sloth. Caio lunged forward, determined to save his friend. He threw the equipment off the top and got down on his knees in front of the cage, looking desperately for the latch. He glanced up and made eye contact with the sloth, trying to communicate that, no matter what, he would never leave her. He knew the poacher was close.

Surprise calmed him as he realized this sloth was not Sandy. This sloth was much lighter than Sandy, with almost blond hair. Relief swirled inside him, but just because this sloth was not Sandy didn't mean it shouldn't be saved. The poachers were coming. Caio undid the latch and grabbed the sloth from within the cage. There was no time to let the animal make its own way out.

With the sloth's claws digging deeply into his arms, Caio scooted off the edge of the truck. As he swung around the cab of the truck, he heard the man shout in surprised anger as he saw all the empty cages. Caio ran to the nearest tree and helped the sloth onto the trunk as high up as he could reach.

"You!" The shout whipped Caio around to face his pursuer. The man stood, chest heaving in anger. Dirt and mud were splattered across his shabby clothing. In his raised hand, he held a machete. Outraged, he lunged forward.

Caio's instincts took over. Blood pumped into his muscles. He ran toward the man. The poacher hesitated, confused. His split-second pause gave Caio enough time to launch off of his leg and kick the man square in the chest with the same movement he had used in dozens of soccer games. He felt a sharp pain in his calf as he kicked out, but he ignored it, and the man, overwhelmed with the force of Caio's kick and the weight of the machete, toppled backward onto the forest floor.

Caio didn't stick around.

Before the poacher landed on the ground, he was running through the forest. Without watching for the branches and bushes in his path, they whipped across his face and arms, sometimes cutting them open. Caio glanced back over his shoulder every once in a while, making sure he wasn't being followed. With his legs on fire and gasping for breath, Caio didn't slow down until he was outside the forest.

Caio panted and stopped. He couldn't help smiling. He let out a celebratory whoop as he came upon the path home.

His mother was setting their table for dinner when Caio walked through the front door. She looked him up and down. She took in his sweaty, dirty clothes and the cuts on his face and arms and didn't bat an eye. "How was soccer today, Caio?" she asked pleasantly.

"Great!" he laughed. "I really nailed my last kick!"

12 DIABLO

The golden rays of morning lit up the treetops. The predawn humidity smothered the air, but Diablo was not focused on the weather today. He squinted at the rickety truck in the distance bouncing along the grassy forest floor.

The truck stopped in a group of trees some distance away. Diablo heard the unnatural slamming sounds as humans emerged. Then he saw them moving through the trees. He snarled. They were placing more bamboo traps. He wanted to run across the open field and destroy each one even now.

I told these humans last time never to return, thought Diablo. *They don't belong here. This is my kingdom. Their hunt disrespects everything about our way of life.*

Diablo stalked closer, planning his attack. Then he noticed one man standing apart from the others. He stared at the long, shiny object in the ugly man's hands. His mind flooded with the memory of the last time he had seen an object like that. As a young adult panther, he had been surprised by a hunting party. Only his quick reflexes had helped him survive that day. He was lucky to have only a scar on his shoulder from the encounter. But even now, Diablo remembered the power of those human weapons that spat fire. They were deadlier, and from farther away, than even his own teeth and claws. The humans had a new advantage. This time would have to be different than the last time they had met.

Diablo took deep, slow breaths as he considered other ways to attack. He looked back toward the truck. It was moving again, headed toward him. He was well hidden, so he decided to simply watch for now. Eyes wide to take in every detail, Diablo stayed still as the truck stopped near his hiding spot.

One of the men climbed from the back of the truck. He took off a covering from his head and wiped sweat away. There were more humans in the back of the truck between a few completed bamboo traps—and from some, Diablo heard the cries of small creatures. Diablo saw more straight pieces of bamboo and rope as well. As Diablo watched, several men crawled out of the truck and began to put together more traps.

Only the thought of the human weapon kept Diablo from leaping out and destroying everything in sight. *No human should take small animals from the forest. They should stay in their world,* Diablo thought. *This forest is mine to protect.*

He turned his attention back to the tall, ugly man with the weapon. He had jumped up on the top of the truck, and now he began barking orders. Diablo shifted silently, keeping all the humans in sight. He would wait until they had left to destroy their traps.

The men worked quickly. They formed each box of bamboo, placing a small piece of banana inside to trick small creatures into entering. But the banana was tied to a rope that released a sliding door that snapped into place, covering the opening where the animal had entered. Once the door clicked into place, escape was impossible. It was a dirty, disrespectful trick. Diablo could smell the sour fear from the creatures already trapped in the truck. It was all too easy to imagine his brother as a cub in their place. *This will not happen in my jungle.*

The sun moved slowly through the sky. Eventually, one of the men shouted, and the men stopped their work. The ugly man with the weapon remained on one side of the clearing. The other workers gathered near each other. They began drinking water from containers in the shade of a nearby tree. Diablo's keen ears heard them talking.

"Wow, a hot one today."

"Yeah, it's a scorcher. Too hot for me, but I really need the money."

"The money is better with this job than others I have had."

"Yeah, the money is great. I was lucky to get this job. Since I got out of prison, no one will hire me."

Diablo could not understand the humans' words, but it was clear from their quiet tones that they did not sense him. They did not smell him. They were unafraid and inattentive to the dangers of the jungle.

"What were you in for?"

"I needed some tools, so I took some, but I got caught. I tried to pay for them after I was arrested, but they stuck me in prison for six months anyway."

"Do we get paid today?"

"It depends on how many animals we capture. We get a bonus if we trap or kill the wild panther that attacked us last time we were here."

"A panther, really? I didn't sign up to be eaten by a panther!"

Diablo recognized their tone. He had heard it before. They were speaking of him. A note of anxiety—if not of fear—came into their scent through the air. *Good.*

"Yeah, we were putting out traps like we are today, and he came out of nowhere. Surprised us. We barely made it out alive. That's why he has a gun today."

One of the men pointed at the ugly man with the weapon. Diablo understood. The humans had brought it for fear of him. They were prepared to defend themselves.

"Can he shoot straight? He seems to drink a lot. I don't want him shooting me instead of the panther!"

"It's relatively safe out here. The psycho panther is the one we have to watch out for."

"Who really cares about these animals? It's not like they can fight back or anything."

"I'm glad we have a couple already in those traps. I want money today."

The humans finished with their water break. The conversation stilled. In the quiet, Diablo could hear the shrieks of one of the trapped creatures in the truck.

"The baby monkey keeps whining," one of the humans said. "Someone needs to go shut it up. It's annoying!"

"Yeah, if you shake the cage, it scares them and helps keep them quiet. Just keep them alive. That's the only way we get paid."

The men returned to work. Together, they got much done in a short time. Diablo snarled but stayed quiet.

They think they are so strong in troops, in herds. Like monkeys, like prey. They rely on one another to defend themselves, but without the "gun," they are helpless. Alone, they are weak and easy targets.

One by one, the humans hid the traps, blending them in to the jungle under leaves and bushes. Diablo waited. Today was not a day for revenge. Today, he would teach a simple lesson—and protect the other animals in the jungle. It would be risky, especially considering the gun. But he was determined to put an end to poaching in his kingdom. It was his duty to face the danger if he called himself king.

The workers began moving back toward the truck. One of them neared the trunk with its trap, already carrying one small monkey. The worker seemed to laugh at the caged animal. The monkey whimpered, banging on the cage with his fist. He was begging for mercy. But the human merely picked up the cage. He shook it, and the monkey banged against its side, crying in pain and fear.

Enraged, Diablo flew from his hiding spot with a tremendous roar. The worker torturing the monkey threw the cage back into the truck. He fell to his knees, quivering at the sight of a two-hundred-pound panther flying in the air toward him. Seeing an escape, he quickly climbed underneath the truck for protection.

Diablo swatted at him with no success. He stood up again and scanned the scene, looking for the gunman. He did not see him. He roared again. The other workers scrambled to run away from the truck and into the jungle.

Diablo moved toward the nearest trap. He raised his right front paw and crushed the wooden trap into bits with one powerful blow.

And then, behind him, he heard the sputter and cough of the truck as it started. The man underneath it had climbed inside while Diablo's back was turned. It roared away in a shower of dirt and grass. Unfinished traps and bamboo sticks came flying out of the back of the truck. It swerved to miss a tree and headed away from the area.

Diablo immediately turned toward the truck. He started to run after it. Inside, he saw the fear on the driver's face. A strange noise like a panicked bird came from the truck. Uncertain, Diablo slowed, looking around for danger. As he slowed, humans came out of the trees again, screaming. They jumped onto the moving truck. Some landed in the back and began to throw pieces of bamboo toward Diablo.

The strange honking noise was harmless! Not a weapon, just a warning. Diablo sped up. The truck was going faster every second. He had to catch it. A shot rang out. A missile whistled past Diablo's head. He couldn't sense its source. He had just moments to catch up to the truck. Diablo kept going.

Another worker ran out from the jungle toward the truck. Diablo heard the voice of the man with the weapon shouting from a different direction, "Get out of the way! You're blocking my view of the panther!"

The running worker looked up and saw Diablo. He panicked, lost his balance, and fell to the ground. Diablo felt a twinge of anxiety. The human with the gun could see him. He remembered all too well how it had been the day he had escaped, wounded, from a similar weapon. A puma that had been trespassing upon his hunting grounds, stalking him for a fight, had been hit instead. She had been killed in one shot.

It was no matter. He was committed now. Diablo dismissed the human with the gun and sprang toward the truck.

In midair, Diablo saw the human with the weapon. He held it against his shoulder, pointing the end in Diablo's direction. He fired. The sound seemed oddly muted this time. Diablo sensed the path the projectile would take and leaned to the right to avoid a direct impact.

He felt a stinging, burning pain in his back leg and landed on the front of the truck awkwardly. Beneath him, the truck turned quickly. Diablo's claws scrambled to maintain his balance on the metal surface, and he flew off toward a group of trees.

Stunned and in pain, Diablo climbed slowly to his feet. He could feel the blood running down his back leg. He turned his head to see the truck driving off into the distance—with workers retrieved from the forest.

Diablo roared out his pain and anger. He began to run again, attempting to follow the truck once more. But within seconds, he knew his leg injury would be enough to keep him from catching it.

Diablo slowed and gave up the chase. He turned around and began to limp toward the area where the traps had been placed. His leg throbbed with every step.

Diablo rounded a tree and stopped in surprise. One of the workers had been forgotten! He carried a finished trap in his hands. Instantly, the worker tried to use the trap as a weapon. He swung the bamboo box toward Diablo. Diablo smashed it with his front paw. Panther and human tumbled to the ground. Diablo stood painfully and realized his front leg was caught inside the trap. Yowling, he raised the front leg wedged inside the trap and pounded it on the ground until it broke away.

As Diablo struggled to free himself, the poacher fought to rise and run away. He was unhurt, but too panicked to move. He made it to his knees, but the fear of death overtook him. His legs buckled.

Free of the trap, Diablo leapt toward the man. The human scrambled for a loose piece of bamboo—a remnant of the trap. He swung it at Diablo's nose and hit hard. But the force of the blow sent the man to the ground again. Diablo landed on top of him. He felt his claws rip into the man's shoulder, and the man screamed under Diablo's weight. Red colored the human's coverings as blood gushed from his left arm.

Diablo swatted the bamboo from the man's hands and sank his teeth into the man's right leg. He knew the man would not live long. He raised his head and watched as the man, eyes dimming, reached inside his shredded shirt. He pulled a small, shiny cross from his chest. He rubbed it between his fingers, mumbling some final words.

Diablo wondered if the man had a family as he watched the shiny object slip from the human's fingers. At any rate, his trespass into the jungle, the disrespect he had shown to its creatures, had been avenged. Diablo roared as the man closed his eyes for the last time.

He stared off into the distance toward the rumbling as the workers' truck rolled farther and farther away. He promised himself that it would be worse if they ever returned.

13 CAIO

Caio awoke with a start from a dream of Sandy, cages, and a rusty red truck. His right calf throbbed painfully.

He sat up and stretched. At times, he had panicked yesterday, but now that he was awake, he smiled when he thought of what he had done. He remembered the look in the tiny monkey's eyes when it had been set free and how satisfying it had been to kick the poacher.

But he had paid for his heroics. Caio glanced down at his leg beneath the sheet. The pain he felt in his right calf now was more than cramps from the run. After dinner last night, after he and Ricardo had gone back to their room, he had discovered blood had soaked right through his sweat-stained pants. When he had kicked out at the poacher, the man's machete had nicked his leg. He had tried to tell Ricardo the stain was mud and had excused himself to bandage the leg. He wasn't sure if Ricardo had believed him.

Now, Caio peeled back the sticky bandage to get a better look at the injury. Thankfully, the wound wasn't too deep. The cut was long, running all down his calf and curving slightly as it neared his foot, but if he kept it clean and bandaged, it should heal well, and he wouldn't need to tell his family, he decided. He didn't want them to worry.

He was proud of his injured leg from fighting the poacher, Caio thought. If he looked past the pain, he had a real battle scar from fighting a bad guy! He felt like a superhero. But as he took a step forward, he winced. Maybe he should take it easy today.

Caio slowly made his way into the kitchen, trying to walk like nothing was wrong. Ricardo sat at the table, chin slumped to his chest and his breathing steady. He had fallen asleep waiting for food. Caio's mother placed a fresh plate of steaming tortillas, eggs, and beans in front of her sleeping son and stepped outside.

Grinning, Caio quietly sat next to his brother and gently pulled the plate toward him. Quick as lightning, he loaded a tortilla and ate a breakfast burrito in a flash. He ate another, keeping an eye on Ricardo. It wasn't until Caio was loading up a third tortilla that Ricardo stirred, sensing something was wrong.

He cracked his eyes open to see Caio eating his breakfast. Ricardo was suddenly wide awake. "Oh no, you don't! That's my breakfast! Get your own!" He seized the plate and began to pull it back toward him.

Caio elbowed his brother in the ribs. It gave him just enough time to load up the last tortilla. He raised the heaping burrito toward his open mouth. Ricardo dug his fingers into Caio's sides, tickling his little brother.

Caio choked, coughed, and laughed. Instinctively, he started to bat Ricardo's hands away. His legs, too, tightened in response, and his right leg brushed painfully along the side of the chair. He grimaced, but Ricardo had already taken advantage of his lowered defenses to seize the last breakfast burrito. He shoved the entire load into his mouth. He turned, mouth brimming with food, eyes gleaming with victory.

Then Ricardo saw the look of pain on Caio's face. He chewed and swallowed quickly, lowering his voice. "I'm sorry, little brother. Are you all right?"

Shooting pains came from the cut on Caio's leg. He shut his eyes tight and lowered his forehead to the table in response.

"I didn't mean to hurt you," Ricardo told him.

Caio sighed. Ricardo felt guilty. He hesitated, then shook his head and looked up. "It wasn't you." Ricardo tilted his head, confused.

Caio looked around to make sure they were alone and scooted his chair back. He lifted the pant leg to show his brother his injury. In hushed tones, he told Ricardo about the poachers.

Ricardo listened intently, eyes wide and staring at Caio's injured leg. When Caio had finished, Ricardo breathed, "You are either one great hero or one stupid boy, and I'm not sure which one. Promise"—he shook his head in emphasis—"promise me you won't ever do that again."

He paused and raised his eyebrows. "Alone," he added.

Caio grinned up at his older brother. Ricardo always had his back. Then his face fell. "Ricardo, I'm worried about Sandy. Do you think you could help me find her?"

Without hesitation, Ricardo smiled and nodded. "Let's change that bandage first."

Twenty minutes later, Ricardo had helped Caio rewrap his wound. Bananas sticking out of their pockets, the two boys set off down the path and into the forest.

"Over here." Caio directed his brother through the familiar surroundings, leading him to the area where he had last seen Sandy. It took them nearly half an hour to locate the solitary sloth. She had been high up in a cecropia tree, sleeping, as sloths are prone to do during the day.

Caio called out to her. “Sandy! My little *pequeño*, come quick! I have a treat for you!”

Sandy stirred, glanced toward Caio, and eventually, slowly made her way down the tree.

Ricardo’s jaw dropped in amazement as he watched the sloth respond to his little brother. He could not believe his eyes. Caio slapped his arm. “Eh, hand me a banana! I promised Sandy I’d give her some next time I saw her.” Ricardo retrieved the fruit from his pocket and handed it over, mouth still agape.

Caio split the end and began to peel the banana, watching Sandy eagerly as she made her way down the tree. He turned, considering his brother. “Hey, Ricardo. Do you want to feed her?”

Ricardo stood for a moment, frozen. “Me? Feed her?” he asked, pointing at his chest. “Will she take it from me?”

Caio laughed and pulled his brother forward. Sandy was near enough now for Caio to reach her. He placed the banana in Ricardo’s hand and moved forward to greet his jungle friend. Caio ran his hand along Sandy's head and back. She closed her eyes, enjoying the feeling.

Caio grabbed Ricardo's arm and brought him forward. "Just break off a small piece and hold it out toward her, like this!" Caio demonstrated. "She'll take care of the rest."

The brothers enjoyed feeding Sandy the bananas they had brought. Ricardo even got up the courage to pet Sandy and feel her textured hair. "This is impossible. You know that, right?" he said over and over again. Caio knew this was something his brother would remember for the rest of his life.

When they finished, Sandy crawled her way back up the tree. They watched silently as she found a comfortable branch to cling to and hid her face. Caio left one final banana on a low-hanging branch, a snack for Sandy while he was away.

Upon arriving home, Caio and Ricardo were surprised to see their father home before sundown. His brows were furrowed, and he looked worried as the boys entered the house.

"Dad!" they said together. "You're home!"

Their father hurried over. "Boys! Where have you been?"

They glanced nervously at each other. "We were out, Dad," Ricardo said. "What's going on?"

Their dad sat with them around the small kitchen table. "There have been rumors of attacks by a black panther around here. I came home as soon as I heard." He looked at Caio as he spoke. He knew how much Caio loved to explore. "Panthers that attack humans are some of the most dangerous and cunning creatures in the jungle. Until it's caught or killed, I do not want you anywhere near the forest. Nothing I have shown you will be useful against it. Understand?"

Caio swallowed and nodded, fear welling up inside of his chest. He was lucky that Sandy had not been found by the poachers. What were the chances that she would be safe from a vicious black panther as well?

14 SANDY

Sandy looked back up as Caio and the other boy—Ricardo—walked away from her tree. They waved one last time as they disappeared into the tree line. It was good, she thought, to find a human she could trust. Caio was her friend. He gave her bananas without traps, just kind words and gentle touches.

She could still smell the sweetness of the banana he'd left for her down below. Caio had peeled part of it for her. Sandy rested as she reached the midpoint in her journey down the tree. The setting sun sprinkled light around her between leaves waving from a soft breeze.

After a moment, Sandy began moving toward the banana again. Then she stopped. For some reason, she felt nervous. She looked around. Nothing seemed unusual, but long ago, Sandy's mother had taught her to listen to her gut.

She decided to take a different path down to the banana. She climbed out on a higher branch. She moved away from the tree trunk to take another look at things.

She had realized some time ago that predators had probably killed her family when she was young. Losing her family had taught her to always pay attention to her surroundings.

Everything seemed peaceful in the forest from her resting place. The birds chattered in the tops of the trees. The leaves swayed in the breeze, but there was no other movement anywhere nearby. Sandy dropped her front claws from the branch and reached back toward the middle of the tree, climbing down to the banana again. She hugged the main trunk with all four limbs as she went.

Sandy reached the branch above the banana. She was looking forward to the treat. She moved toward it, but then the wind shifted, and Sandy stopped moving. She smelled something different—not the banana or anything she had encountered before in a lazy day of sleeping and eating leaves. This smell scared her. The hair on her arms rose up, and Sandy froze with fear. Something was wrong, but she didn't know what.

She hugged the tree to blend in with the bark. What was the new smell? As she pulled closer to the tree, she saw something in the corner of her eye. She was right to be afraid.

The birds screeched overhead, sensing the danger. They flew away in a cloud toward a safer place, but Sandy could not fly. She felt danger closing in. As the black panther leapt toward her with a roar, she ducked her head and threw up her arms to protect herself. If he landed on her or knocked her from the tree to the ground, there would be no escape.

Time seemed to slow for Sandy. Why had she climbed down for the banana? It had been a deadly mistake. Sandy waited for the sharp claws of the predator to sink in.

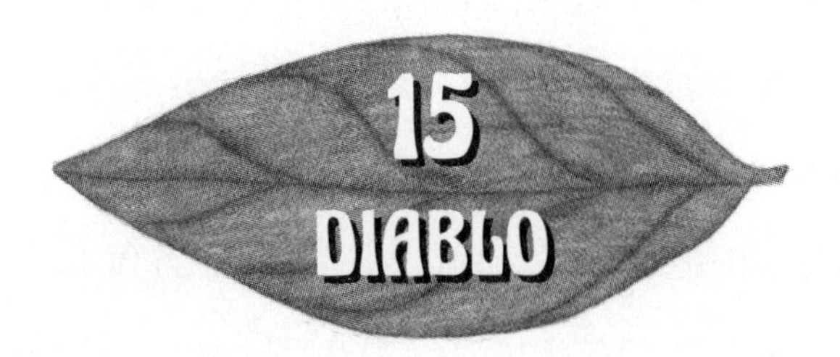

15 DIABLO

The moment Diablo sprang toward the sloth, he knew he had overshot the jump. His front leg ached from where the trap had caught it a few days ago, but it was his back leg that was the trouble. The bullet the poacher had shot at him had only grazed him, but he was weaker. He had tried to move past it and had pushed too hard.

He tried to correct his flight, treading the air with his front and back legs. But he soared past the sloth and smacked into a branch above her with a crashing thud. He clawed and climbed, trying to regain his balance. He clawed at air and let out another roar of helpless frustration.

Gravity pulled at him. He teetered and rocked on the branch for several seconds. Finally, his front right claws caught hold of the wood of the branch. His back feet braced against the trunk. He could smell the sloth below him and knew she was terrified. He needed to act quickly to save this meal.

Now that he was balanced, it was easy for Diablo to turn back toward the tree trunk. He saw the sloth's claws moving upward, partway around the tree. Standing firm with three feet, he slashed at her with his front left paw. She was lighter than he was and faster than he would have expected. If she got too high in the tree, he would have much less of a chance of catching her.

The next few seconds would be critical. They would mean survival for the sloth and another day hungry for Diablo—or a fulfillment of the law of the jungle.

Diablo hit at the tree trunk with his powerful paw. He tried to catch the sloth's claws and throw her to the ground. Grounded, she would be easy prey. Her claws gripped the bark firmly and held her steady. She climbed still higher and further around. Diablo realized her strategy was to stay on the opposite side of the trunk as she climbed, making it difficult to chase her.

With every passing moment, there was less of a chance that Diablo would succeed. To regain an advantage, he crouched down for another jump. His back leg throbbed in protest. Diablo took a breath, focusing on a limb higher up in the tree. He tried to imagine the force he would need. He did not want to repeat his mistake.

Diablo roared and launched upward toward the open limb. The branches quivered as he jumped from branch to branch. Halfway around the tree, he saw the sloth freeze. Her eyes were wide with fear.

This time, Diablo landed with remarkable accuracy. It was time to enjoy today's meal. Hunger gnawed in his gut, and he snarled a warning to the sloth. He moved toward the tree trunk, looking for the branch she was climbing on.

On the trunk, her claws disappeared. *I've won*, Diablo thought. He looked down, expecting to see a sloth falling toward the ground. He blinked, then let out a frustrated breath. She was still in the tree.

Moving around the tree trunk, Diablo saw the sloth had moved out toward the edge of the branch.

Their eyes met. He was ten times larger than she, but as she looked back at him, he was confused at how determined she looked.

She shifted, and the branch beneath Diablo swayed. It was dangerous for him to have chased her so high, but he had to succeed. He had separated and isolated his prey and was moving in for the final kill. He stepped onto the branch she hung on and felt it wobble beneath him, but victory was within his grasp. He moved closer to her, focusing intensely on his prize. He crouched, and the branch began to shake wildly. But Diablo felt confident. He measured the jump between him and the sloth. When he leapt on her, the branch would break. Both hunter and hunted would tumble to the ground. He would survive the fall. The sloth would not.

The sloth closed her eyes. She could not outrun him. She knew this would be the end. Her claws tightened around the branch—but he did not see the panic he expected in her face.

He narrowed his eyes at her, steadied his paws, took another breath, and sprang. As he leapt, he

saw the sloth release the branch, as if to surrender. He glanced toward the ground, checking where they would land—and realized what was beneath them on this side of the tree.

A spike of panic filled Diablo, and he glanced back at the sloth, only to see she had not surrendered at all. Instead, she had simply stretched back, reaching down to the branch just below her. All that was left of her on their branch was her back claws.

Diablo jabbed frantically with his front paws toward the sloth's back claws. He tried to maneuver in midair toward another landing spot. His front paw grazed the place where the sloth had been but was no longer. There was a deafening *crack*, and with a roar of despair, Diablo fell.

16
CAIO

Caio spent a long, sleepless night. He tossed and turned. He couldn't stop imagining a vicious panther hunting his new friend sloth. Caio kept reminding himself that he had seen Sandy just yesterday. She hadn't seemed to be in danger. But he had a sinking feeling in his gut that he couldn't ignore. The worry and stress that had begun with his father's warning grew every hour, and the darkness didn't help.

He was exhausted when the sun rose. His room lightened, and Caio knew there was no use in staying in bed. Caio threw his legs over the side of his bunk and lowered them to the floor, still careful of his injured leg.

"W-what? Caio? Why are you awake?" Ricardo mumbled. He opened one eye.

"I'm going to find Sandy," Caio said simply. His tone of voice was firm. He would not change his mind. "School can wait. Sandy cannot."

Ricardo sat up quickly and rubbed the sleep from his eyes. "You're going, aren't you?" he said. It was not a question. "I'm coming too. You can't go alone; Dad would kill you."

Caio smiled. As always, his brother was there for him.

They dressed silently and slipped out of the house as the first rays of the sun peeked over the horizon. Caio moved slowly with his cut leg. "You know how dangerous this is, don't you?" Ricardo pointed out in a low voice. "That panther could be anywhere, and you can't run like you usually can right now."

"Sandy can't run at all," Caio replied.

As they got closer to the tree line of the forest, Ricardo stopped. He drew a finger to his lips. "We have to be extra careful today." He looked seriously at his little brother. "Stay low and follow me." He waited for Caio's nod before crouching low and entering the forest.

They moved slowly, careful to avoid stepping on leaves or sticks on the ground. The noise could give them away. Ricardo led Caio from cover to cover, using bushes, tree stumps, and camouflage along the way to keep them hidden. Once, they heard leaves shifting and froze. Ricardo gripped Caio's arm, and they waited until they were certain the noise had been a bird flying away or a small creature in the trees and not something more dangerous.

Caio had difficulty staying crouched. The pressure on his calf as time passed hurt more and more. He ignored it. All that mattered today was finding Sandy.

They finally arrived at Sandy's copse of trees in the forest. Caio looked everywhere, searching for some indication of where Sandy might have gone.

Then Caio's heart stopped. Just ahead, he saw jagged claw marks in a cecropia tree. He gulped and reached for Ricardo. They made eye contact, and Caio nodded at the tree. Ricardo paled when he saw the claw marks.

"It doesn't mean anything yet," he whispered to Caio. "She's a good climber, and she could have gone too high for the panther to reach. Let's keep looking."

Caio nodded. A knot in his stomach tightened. *Please,* he thought, *please let her be OK* .

They followed the panther's trail through the cecropia copse where he had jumped and landed again, repeatedly scarring the bark. Caio was sure the black panther had been here. He frowned. They were close to the place where he had dealt with the poachers before. He had not realized how close Sandy had lived to their hunting grounds. Was there more than a panther in the forest for him and Ricardo to worry about?

They continued, alert and searching high in the treetops for Sandy. As Caio searched, he realized that the forest was silent. His eyes landed on an empty nest. He couldn't hear monkeys or birds nearby. That meant predators. Caio bit his lip but didn't tell Ricardo. *It could be poachers*, he reasoned. *They won't* really *hurt us. Probably.*

Then he saw it—something moving in the corner of his eye. Caio whipped his head toward the motion.

It appeared to be a spot overgrown with moss, but Caio knew better.

"Sandy!" he exclaimed. Ricardo ran with him toward her tree. The timid sloth poked her head out further upon hearing Caio's voice. She moved as if to head down the tree—but hesitated.

"Ricardo! I think she's still nervous about the panther." Caio stood tall, determined. "I'm going up there," he decided.

Ricardo could play soccer and run as well as Caio could, and he was better in school, but he had never been able to climb like his little brother. He looked down at Caio's leg. "Can you make it on that leg of yours?" he asked.

"Yes," Caio said defiantly. Without waiting for a response, he hoisted himself up on a lower limb of the cecropia tree. His leg throbbed and slowed his progress, but he was more worried about Sandy than he was about his leg.

Sandy seemed to understand what was happening. No longer hesitating, she began to climb down toward Caio.

They moved toward each other, slow and steady, until they came to the same branch in the middle of the tree. Caio reached his hand toward Sandy and waited, not wanting to frighten the timid sloth. She sniffed his outstretched hand.

Caio laughed. "Are you seriously looking for a banana at a time like this?" He patted her head a few times and then sat very still. She moved forward to sniff his face and hair.

Ricardo was getting nervous down below. The longer they stayed, the greater chance there was they would be caught—by a panther or by poachers. "Caio! We have to go!" he called.

Caio reached for Sandy. He wasn't sure how she'd respond, but she seemed to understand. She climbed closer. Caio reached for her forearms and placed them around his neck. With her arms in place, Caio reached for her legs and wrapped them around his waist. Caio held his breath for a moment, then, when he was sure she wouldn't move, he began to climb back down.

With Sandy clinging to him, climbing down was much more difficult than it had been to climb up.

Caio stopped on each branch to catch his breath and gather his strength. His injury burned, and his arms ached from the climb and Sandy's weight.

A growl ripped through the air then. The black panther was near! Caio froze with terror. His wide eyes found Ricardo's. His brother had his finger to his lips. He crouched silently below, but didn't move, waiting for Caio and Sandy.

The panther snarled a second, then a third time. Caio tilted his head and then smiled. "We're OK," he said, relieved. "He's not getting any closer to us!"

"How on earth could you possibly know that?" Ricardo snapped.

Caio lowered himself carefully from the last branch and landed softly on the damp earth. "The growls," Caio said matter of factly. "They're still as far away as when they started."

Another growl rang through the jungle. "Come see!" Caio called, walking toward the sound.

"Caio!" Ricardo tried to grab Caio's shirt, but Caio was too quick for him.

He walked into a nearby clearing. "I recognize this place," he said. He frowned. Tire tracks on the ground, a broken crate nearby told him that this was the very same clearing where he had freed the animals from the poachers two days ago. His attention was drawn to a cecropia tree on the edge of the clearing, and now Caio realized that he and Ricardo had been to its other side just the day before.

He looked up and pointed.

A branch a little further than halfway up the tree told the whole story. It had been broken in two, snapped with the weight of a creature far too big for it. On the remaining bark were the same claw marks Caio and Ricardo had followed all the way out here, evidence of a less successful landing. And beneath the tree—

Ricardo and Caio took in a breath together. At the foot of the cecropia tree, on this side of it, was a large, man-made hole—the poacher's pit Caio had uncovered the day his leg had been injured. As they walked closer, Sandy's arms tightened around Caio's neck.

Caio and Ricardo peeked over the edge of the pit. A guttural snarl sounded from inside. Far below, a black panther prowled the edges of the pit, his fur thick with mud—and, in some places, blood. His muscles twitched as they watched. He looked exhausted. When he saw them, he leapt at the edge, but the sides of the pit were slick with mud, and he slid back into the hole, defeated.

Caio turned, smiling triumphantly up at his brother. "See?"

Ricardo's jaw had dropped. He looked from the trapped panther to Caio to the clinging sloth. He shook his head. "Sandy, you're one lucky sloth."

EPILOGUE

Sandy yawned. Her tongue rolled lazily out of her mouth. Like the day her family had been taken, her life had changed again. This time, she thought it was a change for the better.

Caio had carried her all the way home, sheepishly greeting his parents outside of their home. They had asked him a lot of questions when they had seen him coming from the forest, and even more when they had seen Sandy. They had decided Sandy could stay in the cecropia near Caio's house. An older human—Caio called him "Dad"—would notify something called the Wildlife Animal Center about the panther.

Sandy shuddered at the memory of the black panther. That had been a close call.

She spun her head slowly around, keeping a look out for Caio. It was past her bedtime, but she knew Caio would only just be on his way to school.

She yawned again, debating whether or not to get comfortable and rest her eyes while she waited.

"Sandy!" A shout came from beyond her sight. "Sandy!" Caio shouted again, closer this time. She smiled and climbed lower down the tree to greet her little human friend. "I've got a banana for you," he said. "But I have to hurry today!"

Caio stopped by her tree every day on his way to school to tell her about his life and spend time with her. Sandy loved their daily visits. Sometimes he came after his dinner—before her breakfast—once she was awake, but only if Ricardo came with him.

"I'm running late!" Caio explained as he split open the banana and offered her a piece. "Mom and Dad are still mad that I skipped school that day, even though I think they know that I did the right thing in saving you." He patted her head and continued, speaking fast. "No one at school believes me! I told them about you and about the panther, but they think I'm making it all up!"

He broke off another piece of banana. "Dad said the Wildlife Center would take care of the panther. I'm not sure what they'll do, but they're the good guys, so it will be OK." He nodded as he continued. "Mrs. Moreno is much harder to convince! I didn't think she was going to let me back into the classroom after skipping, but Ricardo talked to her, and somehow it's all OK!"

Caio offered Sandy the final part of the banana. She smacked her lips, thankful, savoring the last of the treat. Caio patted her head as he finished. "I have to go! If I'm late again, Mrs. Moreno might make me get up in front of the class to make a presentation every day I am late! Aaah! Goodbye, Sandy! I'll see you later!" With one last pat, Caio took off running down the path.

Sandy smiled, her stomach full of delicious banana. Her life was no longer in danger. She had lost her original family, but she didn't think she was wrong that she had found a new one with this unusual, two-legged boy and his sibling and parents. She hadn't expected any of it, but it was a wonderful feeling. She drifted off to sleep completely content. The world, she decided, was a beautiful place.

David's enthusiasm for writing was a lifelong desire just waiting to be realized following a successful career in business management. After a life-changing visit to Manaus, Brazil, several years ago, David developed an affection for the people of South America and the inhabitants of the Amazon rain forest. With a passion for animal rescue, David and his wife, Deana, support pet adoption for orphaned and abandoned animals. Sandy is a two-toed sloth that the couple adopted from Guyana, South America, in the winter of 2014. David, Deana, and Sandy reside in North Texas.

Sandy